Sam Sunday
AND THE MYSTERY AT THE OCEAN BEACH HOTEL

By Robyn Supraner   Illustrated by Will Hillenbrand

Viking

ONE

It was Friday. The day before Saturday. Sam Sunday, the world's greatest detective, sat at his desk and moped.

Today was his birthday and nobody had remembered. Not one card. Not one phone call. Not even one balloon.

Friends are like steamrollers, thought Sam. Sometimes they leave you flat.

The phone rang.

Sam picked it up. "So," he said. "You finally remembered my birthday."

"Detective Sunday?" The voice on the other end sounded frightened.

"Who is this?" asked Sam.

The caller whispered, "Come to the Ocean Beach Hotel. Come now, and come alone."

"What seems to be the trouble, ma'am?" said Sam.

But the caller was gone. The phone was as dead as a doornail.

"Since no one remembered my birthday," said Sam, "I will take the case."

It was a rotten day. Cold and windy. The rain hit his car like a spray of bullets. Sam started the engine. He whistled a tune called "Dixie," and the windshield wipers kept time.

TWO

The Ocean Beach Hotel had seen better days. The roof sagged. Shutters clacked in the wind. The whole place needed paint.

Someone was watching from behind closed curtains. Someone who did not want to be seen.

Sam entered the lobby. It was empty.

Then *she* stepped into the room. She was dressed in black from head to toe. Her hands were shaking. She was scared.

"My name is Betsy Babble," Betsy babbled. She grabbed Sam by the arm. "I'm so glad you came," she whispered. "Something very strange is going on." Her perfume made Sam dizzy.

Betsy ran the place. She worked six days a week and slept in the attic. Sam followed her into the pantry. She poured a drink and handed the glass to Sam.

Betsy filled him in: Things were vanishing. The silver. The china. A whole bowl of tulips. And yesterday a rye bread and seven pounds of knockwurst disappeared. Footsteps were heard in the night. The guests were getting nervous. They were packing up, like rats, and checking out.

Betsy handed the list of hotel guests to Sam:

Mrs. Lydia Lacy and her three daughters
Mr. Dan Digger
Cleo and Cornelius Crumb
Colonel Gooldens
Ms. Hester Primm
Donald, the Grand Duke of Denmark

"Hmmmm," said Sam Sunday. "Very interesting."

THREE

Mrs. Lydia Lacy and her daughters, Faith, Hope, and Charity, were sneaking out of the greenhouse. Mrs. Lacy was pushing a wheelbarrow.

"Hold it," said Sam. "What's your hurry, ma'am? Where are you taking those flowers?"

"No place," said Lydia.

"We're innocent," said Faith.

"As lambs," said Hope.

"Forgive them," said Charity.

"Come with me," said Sam. He led them into the parlor, and told them to sit down and wait.

"I've seen those four before," said Sam to himself. "But where?"

FOUR

Mr. Dan Digger was hiding in the hallway. He was holding an old Victrola.

"Stop right there!" said Sam.

"Sez who?" said Dan.

"Sez me," said Sam.

Digger's yellow eyes glared. One of his eyebrows looked crooked.

"I didn't do nothing," he said.

"*Anything*," said Sam. "You didn't do *anything*."

"Right," said Digger.

"Don't be smart," said Sam. He marched him into the parlor, and told him to sit down and wait.

"Those yellow eyes look familiar," said Sam to himself. "Where have I seen them before?"

FIVE

Sam spotted Hester Primm behind a potted palm. She was wearing dark glasses and a diamond ring. A huge basket stood at her side.

"What's in the basket?" asked Sam.

"What basket?" said Hester.

"Give me a break," said Sam.

Hester gave a little jump. "Wherever did that come from?"

Sam opened the basket. It was filled with apricots and peaches and grapes. It was filled with sandwiches and soda.

Hester slammed the lid on his finger.

"I've seen that ring before," said Sam to himself.

He took Hester into the parlor, and told her to sit down and wait.

SIX

Donald, the Grand Duke of Denmark, and Colonel Gooldens were in the billiard room hatching a plot.

The Grand Duke's beard waggled as he whispered. The Colonel kept his head down and looked grim.

"Are you sure the secret is safe?" asked the Colonel.

"What secret?" said Sam, leaping out from behind the door.

"A snoop!" bellowed the Grand Duke. "This is an outrage!"

"Harrumph!" sputtered the Colonel. "Not very sporting of you, old man. Nasty business, this hiding behind doors!"

"I'm bashful," said Sam. "Shy as a clam."

The Grand Duke's face turned red as a radish. "Who is this spy?" he roared.

"We'll see who's the spy," replied Sam.

He hustled them into the parlor, and told them to sit down and wait.

"I've heard that roar before," said Sam to himself. "But where? Where?"

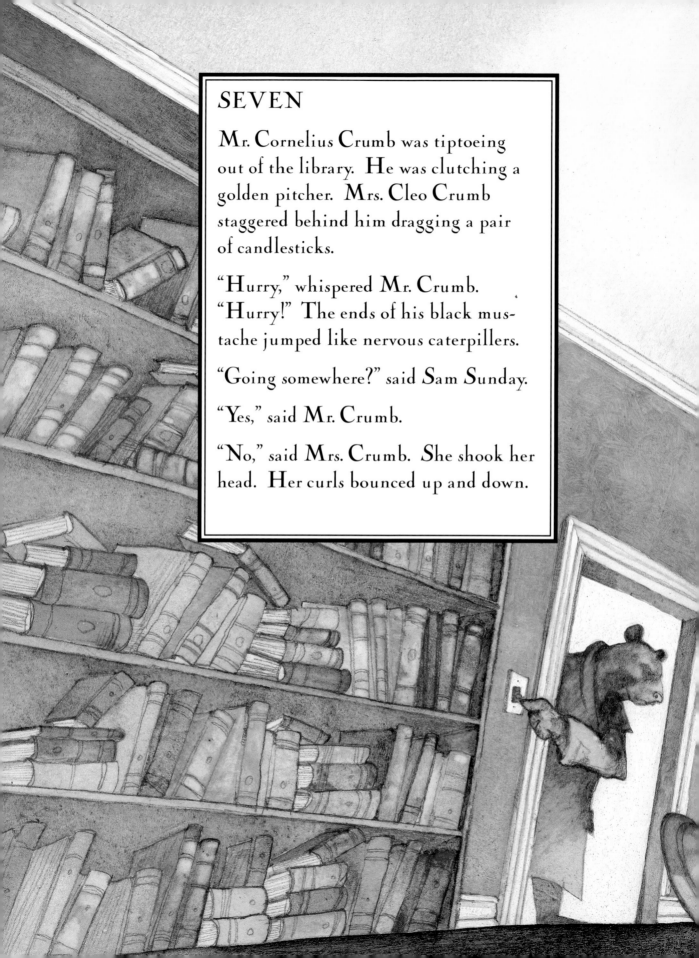

SEVEN

Mr. Cornelius Crumb was tiptoeing out of the library. He was clutching a golden pitcher. Mrs. Cleo Crumb staggered behind him dragging a pair of candlesticks.

"Hurry," whispered Mr. Crumb. "Hurry!" The ends of his black mustache jumped like nervous caterpillers.

"Going somewhere?" said Sam Sunday.

"Yes," said Mr. Crumb.

"No," said Mrs. Crumb. She shook her head. Her curls bounced up and down.

"We thought—" they began.

Sam stopped them. "The trouble is, crooks never think."

He shooed them into the parlor, and told them to sit down and wait.

"I've seen those bouncy curls before," said Sam to himself. He tried to remember where.

Now Sam had everyone seated in the parlor. Everyone but Betsy Babble. Sam went to find her, but she was gone.

EIGHT

"I smell a flimflam," said Sam. "It is time to start asking questions."

He hurried back to the parlor. Good night, Louise! It was empty! The suspects had vanished like soap bubbles.

"So," said Sam. "The plot thickens." He searched everywhere, but no luck. Then he saw a door. It was smooth and shiny. Slick as a nightstick. Above it was a sign that said BALLROOM.

Sam cracked it open. The room was dark. Something rustled. He heard a sneeze.

Then the lights blazed on.

There were Lydia Lacy and her daughters and Betsy Babble and Mr. and Mrs. Crumb and Colonel Gooldens and Hester Primm and Dan Digger and Donald, the Grand Duke of Denmark.

They threw down their disguises and shouted, "SURPRISE!"

And there they were, his friends, laughing and clapping and wishing him a happy birthday.

There were presents and a birthday cake and music.

And there was Betsy Babble, whose real name was Cynthia Green—an out-of-work actress who was just helping out.

"We really fooled you," said the Grand Duke.

"Not really," said Sam.

"Come on," said Hester. "You couldn't have figured it out."

"A piece of ham," said Sam, with a wink.

Cynthia giggled. "You mean a piece of cake."

"Don't mind if I do," said Sam.

And he did.

Outside, the rain had stopped. Stars peeped out like fugitives. And the moon, like a happy cop, grinned in a cloudless sky.

To Leon, my lion,
the light of my life.
R. S.

To Ian, my son, born February 22, 1995, who has brought wonder, joy,
and adventure to my life, as he now investigates a world mysterious and new to him.
W. H.

VIKING
Published by the Penguin Group
Penguin Books USA Inc., 375 Hudson Street, New York, New York 10014, U.S.A.
Penguin Books Ltd, 27 Wrights Lane, London W8 5TZ, England
Penguin Books Australia Ltd, Ringwood, Victoria, Australia
Penguin Books Canada Ltd, 10 Alcorn Avenue, Toronto, Ontario, Canada M4V 3B2
Penguin Books (N.Z.) Ltd, 182-190 Wairau Road, Auckland 10, New Zealand

Penguin Books Ltd, Registered Offices: Harmondsworth, Middlesex, England

First published in 1996 by Viking, a division of Penguin Books USA Inc.

1 3 5 7 9 10 8 6 4 2

Text copyright © Robyn Supraner, 1996   Illustrations copyright © Will Hillenbrand, 1996   All rights reserved

LIBRARY OF CONGRESS CATALOGING-IN-PUBLICATION DATA
Supraner, Robyn.
Sam Sunday and the mystery at the Ocean Beach Hotel / by Robyn Supraner ; illustrated by Will Hillenbrand.   p.   cm.
Summary : Annoyed that his friends have forgotten his birthday, detective Sam Sunday
begins investigating the disappearance of some valuables at an old hotel.   ISBN 0-670-84797-6
[1. Mystery and detective stories. 2. Hotels, motels, etc.—Fiction. 3. Birthdays—Fiction. 4. Parties—Fiction.]
I. Hillenbrand, Will, ill. II. Title.   PZ7.S9652Sak 1996   [E]—dc20   95-46305   CIP   AC

Manufactured in China.   Set in Opti Naval.
The art for this book was prepared in graphite on vellum with oils and oil pastels.